LONGMAN ORIGINALS Stage Two
Series editor: Robert O'Neill

My Dear Aunt

and A Morning in London

Donn Byrne

Illustrations by Rowan Barnes-Murphy

D1664829

 LONGMAN

Addison Wesley Longman Ltd
Edinburgh Gate, Harlow,
Essex CM20 2JE, England
and Associated Companies throughout the world

© Longman Group Limited 1972
© Addison Wesley Longman Limited 1997

First published 1972 in Longman Structural Readers
This edition first published 1997 in Longman Originals

Illustrations by Rowan Barnes-Murphy

Set in 10.5/12pt Melior

Printed in China
EPC/01

ISBN 0 582 27393 5

My Dear Aunt

Scene 1

(Harry and Jane are at home. Harry is watching TV. Jane is sitting at the table.)

HARRY *(Looking at Jane)* Come and watch TV, dear.

JANE No, I want to finish these letters. I've written to Aunt Mary and now I'm writing to Aunt Agatha.

HARRY To Aunt Mary and Aunt Agatha?

JANE Yes. Why not? I've written to Aunt Mary and I've said bad things about Aunt Agatha. Now I'm writing to Aunt Agatha and I'm saying bad things about Aunt Mary! I write two letters – but I put the same ideas in them. It's easy!

HARRY Yes, of course it's easy... but is it a good idea?

JANE A good idea? Of course it is! They love my letters! Look, they're old and rich, and one day they will die... and I want their money.

HARRY Well, *I* want their money, too, but...

JANE Oh, Harry, listen! *(She gets up.)* Aunt Mary and Aunt Agatha live in the same town, but they don't meet. They quarrelled. I can't remember the year because I was very young then. But they quarrelled, and now they don't speak. So I can send the same letter to them and they are very, very happy. And one day I'll be happy too – because I'll get their money. Now I want to finish my letter to Aunt Agatha.

(Jane returns to the table and sits down. She writes for some time.)

JANE *(Getting up)* Well, I've finished.

HARRY And have you invited your aunts this month?

JANE Yes, of course I've invited them. But not on the same day!

HARRY And what have you said to them?

4

JANE Do you want to hear? I'll read Aunt Mary's letter to you. *(She reads one of the letters.)* Dear Aunt Mary... How are you, my dear aunt? Are you well? The weather is very bad these days, so take good care. Wear warm clothes... Aunt Agatha takes good care – *of her money!* She doesn't light a fire in her house because she doesn't want to spend any! Oh, that woman! But I don't want to tell stories. It isn't nice. When can you come and visit us? Can you come on March 21st? We want to see you very much. Harry sends his love. I send my love too. Jane.

HARRY And your letter to Aunt Agatha?

JANE The same, my dear, the same! But of course I've written: "Aunt Mary takes good care..." And I've invited *her* on March 28th.

(Jane puts the letters in envelopes.)

HARRY One day you'll put the letters in the wrong envelopes. Your aunts will get the wrong letters and then they'll quarrel with you.

JANE Oh, I take good care... *(She looks at the clock.)* Half-past five already! I must go and post these letters. Then they'll arrive on Monday. Will you come with me?

HARRY Well, I'm watching this game on TV...

JANE Oh, all right. I'll go and post the letters without you. You make some tea. I need a good cup of tea now.

(Jane goes out of the room. She returns in a quarter of an hour. Harry has made the tea and is watching TV again.)

JANE Well, I've posted the letters. I was just in time and the letters have already gone. Oh, I'm tired!

HARRY Sit down and drink your tea, then. *(Jane sits down.)* This is a very good game.

JANE Football again! I don't like football.

HARRY Well, there's a film at half past seven.

JANE A film? That's nice.

HARRY Yes, and it's good, too. I've seen it. It's about a woman… She has a rich aunt and she wants her money. *(Jane looks at Harry but he is not laughing.)* Then one day the aunt gets a letter. There are horrible things in the letter. So the aunt quarrels…

JANE Oh, stop it, Harry! The film isn't about that. *(Harry laughs but Jane does not laugh.)*

JANE You just want to frighten me. You're horrible! Well, you *can't* frighten me. I haven't put the letters in the wrong envelopes.

HARRY Can you be sure?

JANE Of course I'm sure. I take very good care.

HARRY But you can't be sure! And the letters have gone.

JANE *(Getting up)* I'm not going to listen to you, Harry. You just want to frighten me. All right. There's a very easy answer. I'll phone Aunt Mary. I'll phone her on Monday and then I'll be sure.

Scene 2

(Aunt Mary's house. It is Monday morning. Aunt Mary is eating breakfast. Her maid comes into the room. She has a letter in her hand.)

MAID There's a letter for you, madam.

AUNT MARY A letter?

MAID Yes, madam.

AUNT MARY That's nice. *(She takes the letter and looks at the envelope.)* Oh, it's from dear Jane!

(The maid goes out of the room. Aunt Mary is very happy. She opens the letter and reads it.)

AUNT MARY "Dear Aunt… Agatha!" Agatha! Oh, the letter isn't for me. So Jane writes to my sister, too! What has she written? I must see. "How are you, my dear aunt?" Her dear aunt? But I'm her dear aunt! She says that to me. "Take good care." Hm, she says that to me, too!… What's this? "Aunt Mary takes good care – *of her money!* She doesn't light a fire in her house because she doesn't want to spend any." Oh! Oh! The horrible girl! She writes horrible things about me!

(The maid runs into the room.)

MAID Did you call me, madam?

AUNT MARY *(Crying)* No, I didn't call you. It's this letter. It isn't for me. It's for Agatha, my sister. But Jane put the letter in the wrong envelope. And she's written horrible things about me. About me, her dear aunt! *(She takes the letter.)* Listen to this. No, I… I can't read it again. *(She gets up.)* Well, now I know! Now I know! *(She laughs.)* Well, she won't get *my* money!

(Aunt Mary goes out of the room. The maid takes the letter and reads it. She laughs quietly.)

7

Scene 3

(Aunt Agatha's house. Aunt Agatha is standing in the garden. She is talking to a neighbour.)

AUNT AGATHA … and then I must cut the grass because it's a nice day. But come for tea.

NEIGHBOUR Well, thank you, Agatha. Oh, look. Here's the postman. *(She calls to the postman.)* Any letters for *me*, postman?

(The postman looks in his bag and takes out two letters.)

POSTMAN No, not for you. These are for Miss Street. *(He gives the letters to Aunt Agatha.)* Here you are, Miss Street.

AUNT AGATHA Thank you, postman. *(He goes off and Aunt Agatha looks at the envelopes.)* Ah, this is from Jane.

NEIGHBOUR Your niece?

AUNT AGATHA Yes, my niece. She's a very kind girl. She writes very nice letters.

NEIGHBOUR Well, you want to read your letter. And I must go and do some work. *(She moves off.)*

AUNT AGATHA *(Opening the letter and reading it)* "Dear Aunt Mary…" Aunt Mary! But this is a letter for my sister. That horrible woman!

NEIGHBOUR *(Returning)* What is it, Agatha?

AUNT AGATHA This letter! It isn't for me. It's for my sister Mary. *(She looks at the envelope.)* But it has my name and address on it.

NEIGHBOUR Then your niece put the letter in the wrong envelope. You mustn't read it. Put it in the envelope again and return it.

AUNT AGATHA But what does my niece write to my sister? I want to know. I *must* know!

NEIGHBOUR Well…

8

AUNT AGATHA *(Reading)* Oh, it's horrible. My niece writes to Mary about me! Listen! She says: "Aunt Agatha takes good care – *of her money!* She doesn't light a fire in the house because she doesn't want to spend any!" She says that about *me*, her aunt!

NEIGHBOUR So your niece *isn't* very kind.

AUNT AGATHA Kind! She's horrible! I'm not going to see her again. And she won't get my money.

NEIGHBOUR And is that the end of it?

AUNT AGATHA Yes, why not? I don't want to see her again. She and my sister are the same – two horrible people!

NEIGHBOUR But *you* got your *sister's* letter.

AUNT AGATHA Well?

NEIGHBOUR Then *she* got *your* letter.

AUNT AGATHA Ah, of course. So Jane writes horrible things about Mary *and* me.

NEIGHBOUR Why not speak to your sister?

AUNT AGATHA Speak to my sister? No, I can't do that. We quarrelled!

NEIGHBOUR I know. But now you must punish Jane. She has played a game with you and your sister – and you must punish her.

AUNT AGATHA Yes, you're right. Jane must learn her lesson.

NEIGHBOUR Of course I'm right.

AUNT AGATHA All right. I'll speak to my sister. I don't want to speak to her but I must do it. I'll go and phone now.

Scene 4

(Agatha is phoning her sister Mary.)

AUNT AGATHA Hello? This is your sister Agatha. We haven't spoken for a long time, but now I want to talk to you. It's about Jane.

AUNT MARY Have *you* had a letter from her?

AUNT AGATHA Yes, but *I* got *your* letter.

AUNT MARY And *I* got *your* letter.

AUNT AGATHA So now we know! Jane wants our money, so she plays a game with us. In *your* letter she writes horrible things about *me*.

AUNT MARY And in *your* letter she writes horrible things about *me*!

AUNT AGATHA Well then! We must punish her!

AUNT MARY A good idea. But how?

AUNT AGATHA Well, we got the wrong letters, but Jane doesn't know that.

AUNT MARY And we mustn't tell her – yet!

AUNT AGATHA That's the idea! Now, she's invited you to her house. On March 21st.

AUNT MARY She's invited you too. But on March 28th.

AUNT AGATHA So go to her house on March 21st and…

AUNT MARY But I don't want to see the girl again!

AUNT AGATHA But you must! Go to her house on March 21st… and I'll come too!

AUNT MARY On the same day?

AUNT AGATHA Of course. It'll be a nice surprise for her!

AUNT MARY Yes, a very nice surprise.

AUNT AGATHA I'll arrive first. Jane will say: "Oh, Aunt Agatha, you've come on the wrong day!" But what can she do?

AUNT MARY And then I'll come and we'll meet.

AUNT AGATHA Then we'll tell her.

AUNT MARY I'll say: "Jane, you aren't going to get *my* money. I'm going to leave it to a home for children."

AUNT AGATHA And I'll say: "You're not going to get *my* money. I'm going to leave it to a home for cats."

AUNT MARY Cats! Agatha, you can't do that. You can't leave it to a cats' home.

AUNT AGATHA We mustn't quarrel, Mary. Not now.

AUNT MARY You're right. We must punish Jane.

AUNT AGATHA Well, goodbye, Mary. I'll see you on March 21st... Oh, there's one thing.

AUNT MARY Yes, Agatha?

AUNT AGATHA Perhaps Jane will phone.

AUNT MARY Yes, perhaps she will.

AUNT AGATHA Well, don't speak about the letters.

AUNT MARY No, of course not. And I'll tell my maid, too. Goodbye, then.

AUNT AGATHA Goodbye.

Scene 5

(It is Monday afternoon. Jane is phoning Aunt Mary's house. The maid answers the phone.)

MAID Hello? Boxley 405. Yes, this is Miss Street's house.

JANE Oh hello, Dora. This is Jane. Is my aunt at home?

MAID Yes, madam. I'll go and...

JANE *(Quickly)* Er, how is my aunt? Is she well?

MAID Yes, madam. Very well.

JANE Oh, good! And... did she get my letter this morning?

MAID I don't know, madam. She got a letter at breakfast. Perhaps it was your letter. She was very happy this morning.

JANE Oh, she was very happy. That's good.

MAID Yes, madam. Oh, here's your aunt now. *(To Aunt Mary)* It's your niece.

AUNT MARY I'll speak to her, then. *(She takes the phone.)* Jane, my dear! How are you?... Yes, I got your letter, thank you. It came at breakfast.

JANE *(Very happy now)* I wanted to be sure. And can you come on March 21st?

AUNT MARY Yes, of course I'll come.

JANE Come for the day!

AUNT MARY Thank you, my dear, but I can't. I'll come in the afternoon.

JANE At about three, then?

AUNT MARY No, I'll be there at four, Jane. And how is Harry? Is he well?... That's good. Take good care of him... I'll see you on March 21st, then. Goodbye, my dear. *(She puts down the phone.)* Ugh! Horrible girl!

(Jane is very happy. She calls Harry.)

JANE Well, you were wrong! She was very nice to me,
so she didn't get the wrong letter.

HARRY It's a good thing! But who knows! One day…

JANE Oh, stop it. You just wanted to frighten me and
you know it.

Scene 6

*(It is March 21st – the day of Aunt Mary's visit. Jane and
Harry are in the kitchen. They have made plates of
sandwiches. There are some cakes too.)*

HARRY Well, we've finished.

JANE *You* didn't help very much.

HARRY I did. I made some of the
sandwiches.

JANE Made sandwiches! You ate them!

HARRY I only ate two. I was hungry.

JANE Well, I'm hungry, too. What's the time?

HARRY *(Looking at his watch)* A quarter to four.

JANE Already! Aunt Mary will be here at any minute.
I must go and wash my hands. Shall I change
my dress?

HARRY Change your dress? For Aunt Mary? Why?
She won't look at it. She only looks at the
cakes and sandwiches!

JANE Don't say horrible things about my aunt.

HARRY You say them – in your letters.

JANE Oh, stop it. You want to quarrel. I'll go and change my dress. *(Harry is looking at the food. Jane sees him.)* And don't touch that food!

(At that moment they hear the doorbell.)

JANE Oh, that was the doorbell. Aunt Mary's come already.

HARRY Shall *I* go?

JANE Yes, *you* go. No, *I'll* go. You stay here and make the tea. Remember, Aunt Mary likes good, strong tea. And don't touch that food!

HARRY All right! All right!

(Jane runs to the door and opens it. She finds Aunt Agatha.)

JANE Oh! Aunt Agatha!

AUNT AGATHA Yes, it's me, my dear. Am I late?

JANE Late? No, it wasn't that. But you've come on the wrong day, Aunt Agatha. I invited you *next* week!

AUNT AGATHA *Next* week?

JANE Yes, on March 28th.

AUNT AGATHA No, no, my dear. It was March 21st. I'm sure.

JANE But...

AUNT AGATHA I have the letter here. *(She looks in her bag.)* No, it's at home… Well, my dear, I'm here! Aren't you going to invite me into the house? It's cold here.

JANE Yes, of course, Aunt Agatha. Please come in.

AUNT AGATHA And aren't you going to kiss your old aunt?

JANE Yes, of course, Aunt Agatha. *(She kisses her.)* But you've come on the wrong day – and there isn't any food in the house!

AUNT AGATHA Food! Don't worry about that. Don't worry. I don't come only for food. I don't want much – a cup of tea… Shall I come into the kitchen and help you?

JANE *(Quickly)* Er, no, Aunt Agatha. Come into the dining-room. We can't go into the sitting-room because… because we're painting it.

(Jane opens the door of the dining-room. At that moment Harry comes out of the kitchen.)

HARRY Well, I've made the tea, Jane. Oh, hello, Aunt… Agatha!

JANE *(Quickly)* Yes, Aunt Agatha's come, Harry.

HARRY It's a… surprise!

JANE Yes, it is! Well, aren't you going to kiss Aunt Agatha, Harry?

HARRY Er, yes, of course. *(He goes and kisses Aunt Agatha.)* But why are you going into the dining-room? It's cold there. There's no fire.

JANE Well, I can't take Aunt Agatha into the sitting-room. We're painting it. Remember?

HARRY Oh, of course! And the paint smells.

JANE Well, go into the dining-room and sit down, Aunt Agatha. I'll go and get the tea. And perhaps I can find some food, too.

AUNT AGATHA *(Going into the dining-room)* Don't worry, dear. I told you. I only need a cup of tea.

JANE *(To Harry)* Come and help me in the kitchen, Harry.

(Aunt Agatha goes into the dining-room. Jane shuts the door quickly. She goes with Harry to the kitchen. She shuts the door of the kitchen too.)

JANE Oh, Harry! I want to cry! What are we going to do?

HARRY I don't know.

JANE Well, Aunt Mary will be here in a moment. Think! Think!

HARRY I'm thinking! Well, they mustn't meet.

JANE Of course they mustn't meet. Now, Aunt Agatha's in the dining-room so…

HARRY We'll put Aunt Mary in the sitting-room.

JANE And she must stay there! Now, take some tea to Aunt Agatha. Say: "Jane's making a cake for you." Talk to her. But she must stay in the dining-room.

HARRY Aunt Mary will arrive. What will you do then?

JANE I'll take her to the sitting-room and I'll say: "Harry isn't well. He's in bed."

HARRY Is that a good idea? Perhaps she'll want to see me.

JANE I'll stop her. I'll say: "Harry's sleeping." And she doesn't like you very much! Now, take the tea to the dining-room and talk to Aunt Agatha. Don't stop. And remember, I'm making a cake.

HARRY All right.

(Harry takes the tea and goes into the dining-room.)

HARRY Well, here's some tea, Aunt Agatha.

AUNT AGATHA And where's Jane? Isn't she coming too?

HARRY She's in the kitchen. She's making a cake.

AUNT AGATHA Oh, the dear girl! But why? I'm not hungry. Go and stop her.

HARRY No, no, she wants to make a cake for you, Aunt Agatha. There isn't much food in the house and it worries her.

(At that moment they hear the doorbell.)

AUNT AGATHA That was the doorbell. Why not go and open the door?

HARRY *(Quickly)* No, it's all right. Jane will go.

AUNT AGATHA But she's making a cake.

HARRY Er, don't worry... Oh, I wanted to ask you. How is your garden this year? Are your flowers growing well?

AUNT AGATHA Well, not yet. But the garden's going to be a picture! I've planted...

(Jane runs to the door and opens it.)

JANE *(Quickly)* Hello, Aunt Mary. Come in.

AUNT MARY I'm late. *(She comes in.)*

JANE Please don't make any noise. Harry isn't well. He's in bed and he's sleeping.

AUNT MARY Oh, poor Harry!

JANE Yes, he hasn't slept well for two or three nights.

AUNT MARY Have you called the doctor?

JANE Oh, yes. The doctor's seen him. He says... But come into the sitting-room. I'll bring some tea and then we can talk.

(Jane takes Aunt Mary into the sitting-room.)

JANE Now I'll go and get some tea.

AUNT MARY Can't I help you? You're tired, my dear!

JANE *(Quickly)* No, no, you stay here, Aunt Mary.

(Jane shuts the door and goes to the kitchen again. In the dining-room Harry is giving some tea to Aunt Agatha.)

AUNT AGATHA *(Drinking her tea)* Hm, it's very strong.

HARRY Oh, of course. You don't like strong tea. I'll go and get some water.

AUNT AGATHA And I want to see Jane! She mustn't worry about the cake. I want to talk to her.

HARRY All right. I'll tell her. She'll be here in a minute or two, I'm sure.

(Harry leaves the room. He goes into the kitchen.)

JANE Is it all right?

HARRY Well, we talked about her garden. But she doesn't like the tea.

JANE What's wrong with it?

HARRY Well, I made it for Aunt Mary, so it's very strong. I want some hot water. And how's Aunt Mary?

JANE Well, I've put her in the sitting-room.

HARRY But now Aunt Agatha wants to see you!

JANE Tell her... No, I'll take some sandwiches. And I'll talk to her for a minute or two. Then I must go and see Aunt Mary.

(Harry takes the hot water. Jane follows him with a plate of sandwiches. They go into the dining-room.)

AUNT AGATHA Ah, Jane! Why are you making a cake? I'm not hungry. I told you.

JANE It's only a *small* cake, Aunt Agatha.

AUNT AGATHA But come and sit down.

JANE Yes, of course, Aunt Agatha. *(She sits down.)*

AUNT AGATHA *(Eating a sandwich)* Mm, these are good!

JANE Yes, there was some bread and... Oh, the cake! I must go and look at it! Harry, put some hot water in Aunt Agatha's tea!

(Jane runs out of the room. She goes to the kitchen and makes some tea. Then she takes some cake and sandwiches to the sitting-room.)

AUNT MARY My dear! I've been here for a quarter of an hour and I've seen you for only two minutes.

JANE Well, I made these sandwiches – and then I went to the bedroom. I wanted to see Harry.

AUNT MARY Can I see him too?

JANE He's sleeping, Aunt Mary. He needs sleep, poor man.

AUNT MARY I'll only open the door and look.

JANE Er, no. It's not a good idea. *(She puts the plate of sandwiches in front of Aunt Mary.)* Please eat some of these, Aunt Mary. I made them for you. And here's your tea. *(She gives it to Aunt Mary.)*

AUNT MARY *(Eating)* And how is my sister Agatha?

JANE Agatha? Well, she's... the same!

AUNT MARY You haven't seen her, then?

JANE Oh, no! She phones me and... well, I have a friend. She lives in Boxley too and she tells me about Agatha.

AUNT MARY She's a horrible woman!

JANE Yes, I know – but I don't want to talk about her... There are cakes, too, Aunt Mary. Take one of these. *(She holds the plate in front of her aunt.)*

AUNT MARY *(Eating)* Mm, very good, my dear. But you're not eating.

JANE No, I'm not hungry.

AUNT MARY You mustn't worry about Harry. *(She gets up.)* You sit here and I'll...

JANE No, no, please, Aunt Mary. *(She gets up, too.)*

AUNT MARY But I want to see him.

(She goes to the door and opens it. At that moment Harry comes out of the dining-room.)

AUNT MARY Why, it's Harry!

JANE *(Running to the door)* Harry! What are you doing? Why aren't you in bed?

AUNT MARY But he's wearing his clothes and he's got a plate in his hand!

HARRY I...!

(Aunt Agatha comes out of the dining-room.)

AUNT MARY Agatha!

AUNT AGATHA Mary! What are *you* doing here?

AUNT MARY I came for tea! And what are *you* doing here?

AUNT AGATHA I came for tea, too!

AUNT MARY Well!

AUNT AGATHA Well!

AUNT MARY *(To Jane)* So Agatha comes here too! You told me...

JANE I can explain. Please don't quarrel!

AUNT AGATHA Yes, please explain.

AUNT MARY And don't worry. We're not going to quarrel.

JANE Well, I invited Aunt Mary today – and you came today too, Aunt Agatha.

HARRY And we didn't put you in the same room because you quarrel. It was my idea.

JANE I love you, Aunt Agatha, and I love you too, Aunt Mary. I'm your niece and... and you're my dear aunts!

(Aunt Agatha and Aunt Mary laugh.)

AUNT AGATHA And you write letters to your dear aunts too!

JANE I can explain.

AUNT AGATHA *We* can explain!

AUNT MARY You put the letters in the wrong envelopes, my dear.

JANE Oh no! *(She looks at Harry.)*

AUNT MARY I've read your letter to Agatha.

AUNT AGATHA ... and I've read your letter to Mary.

AUNT MARY A very nice game. You say horrible things about me, Jane!

AUNT AGATHA And about me, too!

AUNT MARY And why?

AUNT AGATHA Because you want our money. You want Mary's money…

AUNT MARY … and you want Agatha's too.

AUNT AGATHA But you're not going to get it.

AUNT MARY I'm going to leave my money to a children's home.

AUNT AGATHA And I'm going to leave my money to a cats' home.

(Aunt Mary and Aunt Agatha walk to the door.)

AUNT MARY Well, goodbye, Jane.

AUNT AGATHA Goodbye! Oh, and thank you very much for tea!

(The aunts go out of the house. Jane and Harry stand there. They do not speak.)

A Morning in London

Scene 1

(Bill and Mary Smith are Americans. They have just arrived in London. They are leaving the station.)

MARY Mm, it's a wonderful day! We can go and see the city this afternoon.

BILL Yes, we'll take a taxi to the hotel. We can eat there and then see London.

MARY Wonderful! Can you see a taxi?

BILL Yes, here's one. *(He calls.)* Taxi! Taxi!

MARY It's all right. It's going to stop. *(The taxi stops. Bill puts their things in it. Then they get in.)*

TAXI DRIVER Yes, sir?

BILL One minute. I have the address in my pocket-book. *(He takes out his pocket-book.)* Ah, yes. White's Hotel.

TAXI DRIVER Very good, sir. I know the place.

MARY Go near the centre, driver. I want to see the big shops.

TAXI DRIVER It's all right, madam. Your hotel is near the centre.

(The taxi moves off. Bill and Mary look out of the window.)

MARY It's wonderful! I enjoyed the plane flight. That was nice, too. But I'm going to enjoy London very much. We'll visit places.

BILL And go to plays in the evening.

MARY Yes, I want to see some new plays, too. I have a good friend in London. She's...

BILL I didn't know. Is she English?

MARY No, no. American. She works in the Consulate.

BILL The Consulate! What does she do there?

MARY I'm not sure. She works in one of the offices. She's been here for about five years, so she knows London. I'll phone her this afternoon. Perhaps she can take us round the city.

BILL And tell us about the new plays. *(The taxi stops in front of a hotel.)*

TAXI DRIVER Well, this is your hotel, sir.

MARY We've arrived very quickly!

(Bill and Mary get out. Bill gives some money to the taxi driver.)

TAXI DRIVER Thank you, sir.

(Bill takes their things and they go into the hotel.)

Scene 2

(In the hotel. Bill speaks to the clerk at the desk.)

BILL Good morning. My name's Smith. I wrote to you about a room.

HOTEL CLERK Smith? *(She opens a book and looks in it.)* When did you write, sir?

BILL *(To Mary)* When did I write? I can't remember.

MARY Well, we wrote from America.

HOTEL CLERK Now I remember. Yes, of course we have a room for you. *(She opens a big book.)* Please write your name and address here, sir. *(Bill does this.)*

HOTEL CLERK Thank you. And your passport number, too, sir.

BILL *(Writing)* Two, five, eight… I can't remember it. But wait a minute. I have my passport here, in my pocket.

(Bill puts his hand in his pocket, but he can't find his passport.)

BILL   It isn't here!

HOTEL CLERK   It isn't important, sir. You can do it this afternoon.

BILL   Yes, of course. But my passport *is* important. And I put it in my pocket. I'm sure.

MARY   Perhaps it's in your bag?

BILL   No. I had some money, one or two letters and my passport. And I put them in my pocket. Oh!

MARY   What is it?

BILL   I put them in my raincoat pocket.

MARY   And where's your raincoat? Did you leave it in the taxi?

BILL   No, I didn't have it in the taxi. So I…

MARY   So you left it on the train!

BILL   Yes, I left it on the train…

HOTEL CLERK   Well, don't worry, sir. Just go to the station and you'll find your raincoat there.

BILL   Are you sure?

HOTEL CLERK   Oh yes, sir. They have a Lost Property Office there. Just go and ask. You'll get your raincoat.

BILL   Well, I'll go now. I don't need my raincoat, but my passport is important.

MARY   I'll come with you.

BILL   No, you stay here, in the hotel.

MARY   All right, then.

(Mary goes to their room. Bill returns to the station.)

Scene 3

(Bill has returned to the station. He sees a policeman there.)

BILL Excuse me. I want the Lost Property Office.

POLICEMAN The Lost Property Office?

BILL Yes. I left my raincoat on the train.

POLICEMAN Follow me, sir.

(The policeman goes into the station and Bill follows him.)

POLICEMAN Now, sir. Can you see that office over there?

BILL The one with the big door?

POLICEMAN That's right. Well, that's the Lost Property Office.

BILL Thanks very much.

(Bill goes to the Lost Property Office and walks in. An old man is standing behind the counter.)

BILL Excuse me...

OLD MAN Yes, sir? What can I do for you?

BILL Well, I've lost my raincoat. I left it on the train this morning.

OLD MAN Which train?

BILL I came from Gatwick airport.

OLD MAN Hm, a raincoat. I don't remember a raincoat. But I'll look in the book. Wait a minute.

(The old man brings a big book. He reads the list of things.)

OLD MAN ...radio, hat (man's), book, handbag, dog...

BILL Dog! Did you find a dog on the train?

OLD MAN Well, this was only a child's toy. A toy dog. But we have found dogs on trains. I remember... But I must find your raincoat. *(He looks at the list again and reads.)* Ah, here's a raincoat. What colour was your coat, sir?

BILL Grey.

OLD MAN Then this isn't your raincoat, sir. This one is black. But don't worry, sir. We'll find your raincoat for you. *(He looks at the list again.)* Now here's a second raincoat – and it's grey. Was your coat new, sir?

BILL No, it wasn't new.

OLD MAN And were there things in the pockets?

BILL Yes, there was some money. Not very much. But there were some letters – and my passport. That's the important thing.

OLD MAN Then this is your raincoat. We've put a number on it. Sixty-seven. I'll go and get it for you. *(He goes to the back of the office. He returns with a raincoat and puts it on the counter.)*

OLD MAN Is this your raincoat, sir?

BILL Yes, that's it! Thanks very much. What do I do now?

OLD MAN Sign in the book. Just sign your name here and you can take your raincoat.

(Bill signs his name in the book.)

BILL Er, what do I pay for this?

OLD MAN That's three pounds fifty pence, sir.

(Bill puts his hand in his pocket and takes out some money.)

BILL Here you are.

OLD MAN Thank you, sir. Now, about the things in your raincoat pocket...

BILL Ah, yes. My passport. They're here of course.

OLD MAN We don't leave things in the pockets, sir. We take them out and make a list...

BILL But you have them here...

OLD MAN No, we put them in an envelope. And we send the envelope to the station-master's office.

BILL Ah, so I haven't finished!

OLD MAN That's right, sir. You must go to the station-master's office. Just take this note and you'll get your things. The envelope has your name on it.

BILL And where's the station-master's office?

OLD MAN Go out of here and turn left. It's the third office.

BILL Well, thanks again.

(Bill goes to the door of the office. He is just leaving. The old man calls to him.)

OLD MAN Oh, sir!

BILL *(Turning)* Yes?

OLD MAN Don't you want your raincoat? You've left it on the counter!

Scene 4

(Bill goes into the station-master's office. A man is writing at a desk. He looks up.)

BILL Excuse me, are you the station-master?

CLERK Me? No, I'm only the clerk, sir.

BILL Well, where can I find the station-master, then?

CLERK He's just gone out. Can I help you, sir?

BILL' Well, it's like this. I left my raincoat on the train this morning.

CLERK You must go to the Lost Property Office for that, sir.

BILL I know. I've just come from there. I've got my raincoat, but there were some things in the pockets. They put them in an envelope and sent them here. Look, I've got a note. It has a list of the things on it.

(The clerk takes the note and reads it.)

CLERK Money – three pounds... two letters... passport. Ah, I remember that envelope. It has your name on it. William Smith.

BILL That's right.

CLERK We put the envelope in the safe.

BILL And can I have it?

CLERK Of course, sir – but I haven't got the keys to the safe.

BILL Who's got them?

CLERK The station-master.

BILL And where can I find him?

CLERK Well... why not wait five minutes and he'll come. Ah, it's all right. He's coming now.

(A big man comes into the office.)

CLERK This is Mr Smith, sir.

S/MASTER Mr Smith?

CLERK Yes, sir. We've got an envelope with his things in it. Some money, letters and a passport.

S/MASTER Ah, yes. I remember.

CLERK Well, I need the keys of the safe, sir. We put the envelope in there.

(The station-master gives the keys to the clerk. The clerk goes to the safe and opens it. He takes out an envelope and brings it to Bill.)

CLERK Well, here you are, sir.

BILL What do I do now? Do I sign for this?

CLERK That's right, sir. Here's the book. *(The clerk puts a book in front of Bill. Bill signs his name in it. Then he opens the envelope and takes out the things.)*

BILL Money... letters... But my passport isn't here!

CLERK No passport? *(He turns to the station-master.)* Mr Smith's passport isn't here, sir.

S/MASTER Ah, no. I took the passport out of the envelope.

BILL You took the passport out!

S/MASTER That's right. And I sent it to the police.

BILL You sent it to the police!

S/MASTER Yes, of course. A passport is very important.

BILL Well, you're right. So where do I have to go for my passport?

S/MASTER To the police station. Here's the address. It's very near. *(He writes the address on a piece of paper.)* Here you are, sir. Just go there and ask for your passport.

BILL Thanks very much.

(Bill takes the piece of paper and goes to the door.)

CLERK Sir!

BILL *(Turning)* Yes?

CLERK You've left the envelope here on the desk! With your money and letters.

Scene 5

(At the police station. A police sergeant is sitting behind a desk.)

BILL Excuse me, sergeant. I've come for –

SERGEANT – your passport!

BILL Oh, you know already!

SERGEANT Yes, the station-master has just phoned.

BILL People are very kind! Yes, I've come for my passport.

SERGEANT Well, I'm very sorry, sir. Your passport isn't here.

BILL Not here? Then, where is it? The station-master sent it here.

SERGEANT Yes, but I sent it to the Consulate. The American Consulate.

BILL Oh no!

SERGEANT Wasn't that right, sir?

BILL Oh, it's the right Consulate, of course. But...

SERGEANT Well, it's the right place for a passport. Look, sir. A man loses his passport, so what does he do? He phones his Consulate, of course. Or he goes there. So I sent your passport to your Consulate.

BILL Of course you did the right thing, sergeant. Only
I'm tired! I've been to the Lost Property Office,
the station-master's office, the police station…!
And now I have to go to the Consulate. Well, I'll go
now. Have you got the address? I've only just
arrived in London.

*(The police sergeant writes the address on a piece of paper
and puts it on the desk, in front of Bill.)*

SERGEANT There's one thing, sir. The office there isn't open
now.

BILL Not open? Why not?

SERGEANT It closes for lunch.

BILL When does it open again?

SERGEANT At two o'clock, sir.

BILL *(Looking at his watch)* Hm, an hour. Well, I won't
see London today!

SERGEANT Oh, you will, sir. Listen, go and get some lunch
now. There's a good place near here. Then take a
taxi and go to the Consulate. You'll only be there
five minutes. Then you can go and see London.

BILL Well, I need some lunch after this! Can I phone my
wife from here? I left her in the hotel and she's
waiting for me.

SERGEANT Yes, of course, sir. What's the number of the hotel?

BILL I don't know the number. It's White's Hotel.

SERGEANT White's Hotel. I'll look in the book.

*(The police sergeant opens the telephone book and looks
for the number.)*

SERGEANT I've got it, sir. *(He phones the hotel and waits.)* Ah,
hello? White's Hotel?

BILL … William Smith.

SERGEANT Mr William Smith wants to speak to his wife. All right. *(To Bill)* They're looking for your wife now, sir. *(They wait.)* Yes? She's not in the hotel? Thank you very much. *(He puts down the phone.)* Well, your wife isn't in the hotel. Perhaps she's gone for lunch, too, sir.

BILL Or she's looking for me! Well, thank you, sergeant. I'll go and get some lunch. Then I'll phone again. Now, I've got my raincoat… and the envelope… Good!

SERGEANT And don't forget this, sir. The address of the Consulate. You've left it on my desk.

BILL Ah, thank you very much. Well, goodbye, sergeant.

SERGEANT Goodbye, sir.

(Bill goes out of the police station.)

Scene 6

(It is two o'clock. Bill goes into the American Consulate. A woman is sitting behind a desk.)

BILL Good afternoon. I've come for a passport.

WOMAN Do you want a new passport?

BILL No, not a new one. I've lost my passport.

WOMAN Then you want a new one.

BILL No, I don't. My passport is here, at the Consulate.

WOMAN How do you know?

BILL Because the police sent it here.

WOMAN All right. But you didn't say that! Well, you must see Miss Bell. She takes care of these things. *(She phones.)* Susan, a man wants to see you. He's lost his passport and the police sent it here. His name? Just a minute. *(She speaks to Bill.)* What's your name, please?

BILL Smith. William Smith.

WOMAN *(Speaking to Miss Bell again)* His name's William Smith. Ah, you have his passport, then? Good! *(She puts down the phone and speaks to Bill.)* It's all right. She's just going to bring your passport.

BILL Thank you.

WOMAN Why not sit down? There's a chair over there.

BILL Thanks but I'll wait here. I just want to get my passport!

WOMAN How did you lose it?

BILL Well, it's a long story! I left my raincoat on the train, and my passport was in the pocket. So, I went to the Lost Property Office and I got my raincoat.

WOMAN But your passport was here.

BILL Well, the passport wasn't the only thing in my pocket. There were some letters and some money. They sent those to the station-master's office. He sent my passport to the police.

WOMAN And the police sent it here.

BILL That's right. Well, I was in the police station at one o'clock. But your office wasn't open. So I got some lunch and... here I am!

WOMAN And here's Miss Bell, with your passport.

(Susan Bell comes into the room.)

SUSAN BELL Mr Smith?

BILL Yes, that's me.

SUSAN BELL Well, here's your passport. *(She opens it and looks at the photograph.)* The photograph isn't like you! *(She shows it to the woman at the desk.)* Is it?

WOMAN Not very, but of course…

BILL Well, it's an old photograph.

SUSAN BELL Hm, all right. Photographs in passports are not very good. Here you are, then. *(She gives the passport to Bill.)* Take good care of it now!

BILL Don't worry, I will! Thank you very much. *(Bill says goodbye to the women. Then he goes out.)*

SUSAN BELL These stupid people! How did he lose it? Did he tell you?

WOMAN Well, it's a long story. He left his raincoat on the train and…

SUSAN BELL And just look! He's left his raincoat here! The stupid man! Well, I'll put the raincoat in my office. No! I'll leave it here. I don't want to see *him* again!

Scene 7

(Bill has returned to the hotel. He is in the bedroom. He is sitting on the bed and talking to Mary.)

BILL …he was very helpful… and then we phoned the hotel but you weren't here.

MARY Well, I waited and waited – but you didn't come. I was hungry, so I went out and got some lunch.

BILL Of course. Well, I got some lunch, too, and then I went to the Consulate. And I got my passport! Look! *(He shows the passport to Mary.)* That's the important thing.

MARY Well, now we can go and see London. But it isn't very nice now. That wonderful weather has gone already!

BILL Yes, it's going to rain.

MARY Well, we've got raincoats. *(She looks round the room.)* Bill, where is your raincoat?

BILL My raincoat? I had it. Isn't it here?

MARY I can't see it. *(She looks at Bill.)* Have you lost it again?

BILL Well, I had it in the Consulate. I remember very well.

MARY So you left it there! Oh, Bill, you are stupid!

BILL Well, I don't want to go to the Consulate again. Those women will laugh at me. I'll… I'll buy a new one. I needed a new raincoat. That one was old.

MARY I know! I'll phone my friend and tell her about the raincoat. Then she can bring it.

BILL That's a good idea! Then I won't see those women again.

MARY They won't know about it! Leave it to me!

BILL Thanks, Mary.

MARY I'll go and phone Susan, then.

BILL Susan?

MARY Yes, Susan Bell. *(She looks at Bill's face.)* What's wrong, Bill?

BILL Well…

MARY Oh no! So you've met my friend already!

BILL Yes, she was the girl in the office. She had my passport.

MARY *(Laughing)* And now she's got your raincoat! Well, she's going to laugh, of course!

BILL But do we have to meet her? I don't need that raincoat and…

MARY Oh, come on, Bill! It's not the end of the world! I want to see my friend again – and I want to see London too. It's all right for you! You've seen London already!

READING ACTIVITIES

Before reading

1 Look carefully at the picture on page 3. What are Jane and Harry doing?

2 Do you have a favourite aunt or uncle? What makes this person special?

3 What things must you remember to take with you when you go on holiday to another country? Make a list of the three most important items.

While reading

My Dear Aunt

1 Read Scene 1 first. Why can Jane say bad things to Aunt Mary about Aunt Agatha, and bad things to Aunt Agatha about Aunt Mary?

2 Read to the end of Scene 4 first. Then put these sentences into the correct order.

Jane phoned Aunt Mary.
Aunt Agatha phoned Aunt Mary.
Jane's letters went to the wrong aunts.
Jane wrote a letter to each of her aunts.
The aunts agreed to punish Jane.

3 Now read Scene 6. Draw a plan of Jane and Harry's house. Show where they put the two aunts. Where did everybody meet in the end?

A Morning in London

4 What do Bill and Mary want to do while they are in London? Read Scene 1 carefully and make a list.

5 As you read the rest of the play, fill in the blanks for the map on the next page. It shows where Bill went on his first morning in London.

1 .....station....................

2 ....

3 ....

4 ....

5 ....

6 ....

After reading

1 You have come to a friend's house for a party. But it's the wrong day! What happens when your friend opens the door? Write a short dialogue. You may want to act it with a partner.

2 Think about the people you have met in *My Dear Aunt.* Who would say the following things? Choose the best answers from the box.

"Cats are so much nicer than people, you know."

"What will you do if they get the wrong letters?"

"And now I'll never get their money."

"I agree with you about one thing, Agatha."

"I have a parcel for you, Miss Street."

Harry	Aunt Mary	Aunt Agatha	Postman
Jane	Maid	Neighbour	

3 Mary Smith is sending a postcard from London to her best friend at home in the United States. Write the card, and include a few sentences about:

the weather

their first day in London

their plans for the rest of the holiday

Donn Byrne

Longman Originals are specially written for students of English to read for pleasure. Illustrated in full colour, *Longman Originals* are graded in four stages from beginner to intermediate level, following our internationally established language guidelines.

The first of these two plays is about Jane. Jane has two dear aunts. They are also rich aunts. And they don't like each other. So Jane plays a little game. But will everything work out as she plans?

Bill Smith is an unlucky American tourist in the second play. Find out what happens to him on his first morning in London…

Illustrations by Rowan Barnes-Murphy

 These plays are recorded on cassette.

My Dear Aunt and A Morning in London

Stage 2

LONGMAN

ISBN 0-582-27393-5

Daphne Bruland

Zu: Klaus Mann: Mephisto, Roman einer Karriere

Hendrik Höfgen als Prototyp eines Opportunisten, eines
Kollaborateurs des Nationalsozialismus

Zwischenprüfungsarbeit

VERLAG FÜR AKADEMISCHE TEXTE